做了這本書

WRECK THIS JOURNAL

TO CREATE IS TO DESTROY
搞　　　破壞　　　就是 搞　　　創作

BY　KERI SMITH
凱莉・史密斯　著

U0017499

做了這本書
WRECK THIS JOURNAL

作　　者 凱莉‧史密斯 Keri Smith
總 編 輯 汪若蘭
執行編輯 陳希林、徐立妍
版面構成 陳健美
封面構成 張凱揚
行銷企畫 高芸珮

發行人 王榮文
出版發行 遠流出版事業股份有限公司
地址 臺北市南昌路2段81號6樓
客服電話 02-2392-6899
傳真 02-2392-6658
郵撥 0189456-1
著作權顧問 蕭雄淋律師
法律顧問 董安丹律師

2012年9月1日 初版一刷
2013年7月15日 初版11刷
行政院新聞局局版台業字號第1295號
定價 新台幣250元
（如有缺頁或破損，請寄回更換）
有著作權‧侵害必究 Printed in Taiwan
ISBN 978-957-32-7033-1

YLib 遠流博識網
http://www.ylib.com E-mail: ylib@ylib.com

這也是作者

凱莉・史密斯（Keri Smith），知名藝術家暨作家，其部落格 Wish Jar 每日吸引超過八千人瀏覽，著有《亂糟糟》（2010）、《這不是一本書》（2009）、《如何探索世界》（2008）、《做了這本書》（2007）等與創意相關的書籍。除了為雜誌撰文之外，她也為華盛頓郵報、紐約時報、福特汽車、《時人》雜誌、Body Shop 與 Hallmark 等公司繪製插畫。

《畫畫的52個創意練習》作者卡拉・桑罕推薦！

第一本真正「讓讀者親身參與」的書
第一本真正「讓創意自由發揮」的書
第一本真正突破紙本書限制、提供讀者創意點子，創作個人化作品的書

這本書有洗滌心靈的作用，它讓我可以把對生病這件事的憤恨、怒氣、恐懼、失望，還有所有可怕的情緒通通發洩出來。

——美國讀者Sarah

這本書真的太太太有趣了！它讓我完全脫離舒適圈，使內向的人變得外向。

——美國讀者Erica

坦白說，這本書超出我原本的預期。我不喜歡指南書，但是作者把看似無聊的指南變得處處充滿驚奇。

——美國讀者T. Adlam

本來我以為這本書沒什麼，但照著做之後，卻受到非常大的啟發，書裡非常大膽與革命性的創意，讓我不斷在每個頁面上自由揮灑。五顆星推薦推薦！。

——美國讀者Elizabeth

警告：在你做了這本書的過程中，你全身都會弄得髒兮兮的，到處都沾到顏料，到處都有不知哪裡跑來的東西黏著。你身上會弄濕，而且本書會叫你做一些讓你很……不習慣的事。本書被你做了之後，再也不會平整無瑕，而你可能會感到心疼。不過，透過本書大膽又極具創意的點子，你的人生從此會變得更無拘無束。

還有：本書題獻給全球每一位完美主義者。本書並不保證、擔保或代表（明示或暗示）資料內容一定會讓你覺得有趣。從事創意工作並不表示絕無風險，創意工作者過去之創作績效不保證未來創意之最低產值。從事創意工作可能之風險包含市場風險（政治、經濟、社會變動、匯率、利率、股價、指數或其他標的資產之價格波動）、流動性風險、信用風險、產業景氣循環變動、法令、貨幣、流動性不足等風險，創意工作者宜明辨風險，謹慎投資。創意人因不同時間進場，將有不同之創意績效，過去之績效亦不代表未來績效之保證，創意工作者入行前應詳加考慮。有關創意工作之艱難，已揭露於史上其他藝術家悲苦回憶錄，創意工作者可至國內公開圖書市場或境外圖書資料中心購買相關內容加以閱讀。本書除盡善良管理人之注意義務之外，下一句該寫什麼就不知道了。

THIS BOOK BELONGS TO:
本書的主人是

WRITE YOUR NAME IN WHITE.
請用白色字跡寫下你的名字

WRITE YOUR NAME ILLEGIBLY.
請用無法辨識的字跡寫下你的名字

WRITE YOUR NAME IN TINY LETTERS.
請用超小超小超小字體寫下你的名字

WRITE YOUR NAME BACKWARD.
請把你的名字倒過來寫

WRITE YOUR NAME VERY FAINTLY.
請用非常非常淡的筆跡寫下你的名字

WRITE YOUR NAME USING LARGE LETTERS.
這裡用粉大粉大超巨大的字體寫下你的名字

ADDRESS
你家地址在這裡

PHONE NUMBER
你家電話是這個

*若有善心人士發現此書，懇請翻到書內任何一頁，按照該頁指示完成，然後將本書寄還。

預備起

1. 不管走到哪，這本書就帶到哪

2. 每一頁的指示都要遵照辦理

3. 不要管頁碼順序（這本書根本沒頁碼好嗎）

4. 每一頁的指示都可自由詮釋

5. 勇敢實驗吧（打破你的常規）

materials 所需素材

點子　　　　　　味道
口香糖　　　　　雙手
膠水　　　　　　細繩
泥土　　　　　　球
口水　　　　　　脫離常軌
水　　　　　　　即興
天氣　　　　　　照片
垃圾　　　　　　報紙
植物　　　　　　白色的東西
鉛筆／筆　　　　辦公用具
針與線　　　　　蠟
郵票　　　　　　外面撿來的東西
貼紙　　　　　　釘書機
很黏的東西　　　食物
小棍子　　　　　茶／咖啡
湯匙　　　　　　情緒
梳子　　　　　　恐懼
扭線環　　　　　鞋子
墨水　　　　　　火柴
顏料　　　　　　生物
小草　　　　　　剪刀
清潔劑　　　　　膠帶
油漬　　　　　　時間
眼淚　　　　　　機緣
蠟筆　　　　　　決心
　　　　　　　　尖銳物

ADD YOUR OWN PAGE NUMBERS.

自己寫頁碼

STARTING HERE

寫在這裡

CRACK THE SPINE.

把書背弄裂開

LEAVE THIS PAGE
BLANK
ON PURPOSE.

故意讓這頁留白

STAND HERE.
(WIPE YOUR FEET, JUMP UP AND DOWN.)
站上來（用這頁擦腳，在這頁上下跳）

POUR, SPILL, drip, SPIT, fling YOUR COFFEE HERE.

在這頁用咖啡澆、潑、滴、噴、甩

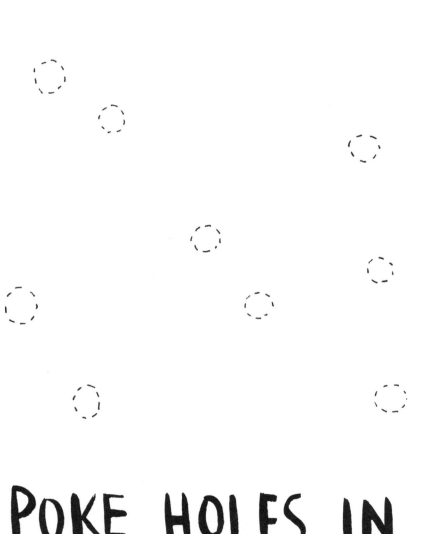

POKE HOLES IN
THIS PAGE USING
A PENCIL. 用鉛筆在這頁上面玩戳戳樂

DRAW FAT LINES AND THIN.

PUSHING REALLY HARD WITH THE PENCIL.

畫粗線，畫細線，拿鉛筆用力畫

THIS PAGE IS FOR HANDPRINTS
OR FINGERPRINTS. 把手弄髒，在這裡蓋手印，蓋指印
GET THEM DIRTY THEN PRESS DOWN.

COLOR THIS ENTIRE PAGE.

把這整頁塗滿

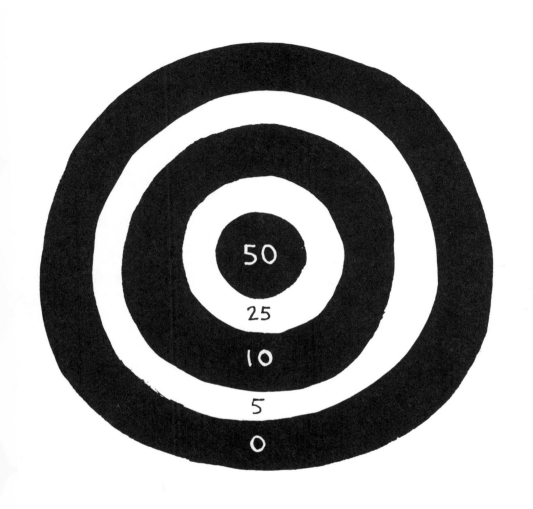

THROW SOMETHING

A PENCIL, A BALL DIPPED IN PAINT.

把這頁當靶，丟東西上去！（可以用鉛筆當飛鏢，也可把球沾顏料來扔）

把葉子壓在這裡（也可以用其他外面撿來的東西）

PRESS LEAVES AND OTHER FOUND THINGS

SCRATCH

拿尖銳物在這裡刮擦

USING A SHARP OBJECT.

DO SOME RUBBINGS WITH A PENCIL.

用鉛筆做拓印

SCRIBBLE WILDLY, VIOLENTLY, with RECKLESS ABANDON.

狂畫，猛畫，盡情畫

TEAR STRIPS 扯開！撕成一條一條的
RIP IT UP!

用膠水、釘書機或膠帶，把這兩頁黏起來

draw lines

ON THE BUS, ON A

While IN MOTION.
TRAIN, WHILE WALKING.

FILL THIS PAGE WITH CIRCLES.

用圓圈填滿這頁

Document your dinner.

RUB, SMEAR, SPLATTER YOUR FOOD.

USE THIS PAGE AS A NAPKIN.

CHEW ON *this.*

咬這裡

---

*WARNING: DO NOT SWALLOW.

---

*警告：禁止吞嚥

把這頁捲成漏斗，拿來喝水

MAKE A FUNNEL.

DRINK SOME WATER.

1. CUT OUT.

沿線剪下

2. ROLL & TAPE.

捲成形，用膠帶固定

3. ADD WATER & DRINK.

拿來喝水

TEAR OUT

CRUMPLE.

揉成一團

沿線撕下

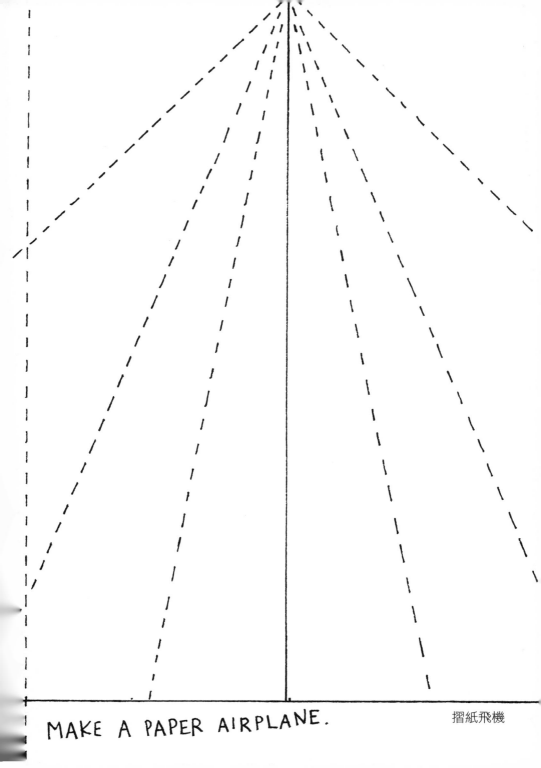

MAKE A PAPER AIRPLANE.

摺紙飛機

WRAP something
WITH THIS PAGE.

like this
示意圖 this

拿這頁來包東西

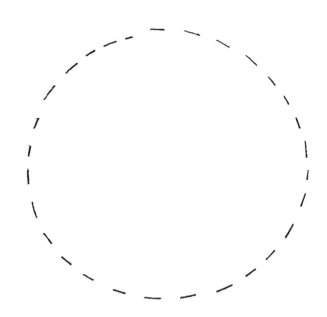

TONGUE PAINTING

1. EAT SOME COLORFUL CANDY.

2. LICK THIS PAGE.

舌繪：1. 先吃有色素的糖果　　2. 再舔這裡

在這裡把同一個字寫一千萬遍

WRITE ONE WORD

OVER AND OVER.

TIE A STRING

TO THE *spine* OF

THIS BOOK.

SWING

WILDLY

LET IT HIT THE WALLS.

拿一條細繩子，綁在書背上。
用力晃動，讓這本書去撞牆。

PICK UP THE JOURNAL WITHOUT USING YOUR HANDS.

拿起這本書。禁止用手

爬高高，把手上的書扔下來

把這頁拿去做堆肥，觀察它變成腐土的過程

compost this page.

watch it deteriorate.

DO A really UGLY
(USE UGLY SUBJECT MATTER:
A BADLY DRAWN BIRD,

DRAWING

GUM, POO, DEAD THINGS, MOLD, BARF, CRUD.)

畫一幅醜斃了的畫（使用醜斃了的素材：咬過的口香糖、糞便、生物屍體、醜斃了的鳥圖、發霉的東西、嘔吐物、渣滓）

此頁
放一些
很黏很黏
的東西：
蜂蜜、
口香糖（要先咬）、
糖漿、膠水、
棒棒糖、
棉花糖

假裝你一邊講電話，一邊在這個信封背面，隨便亂畫

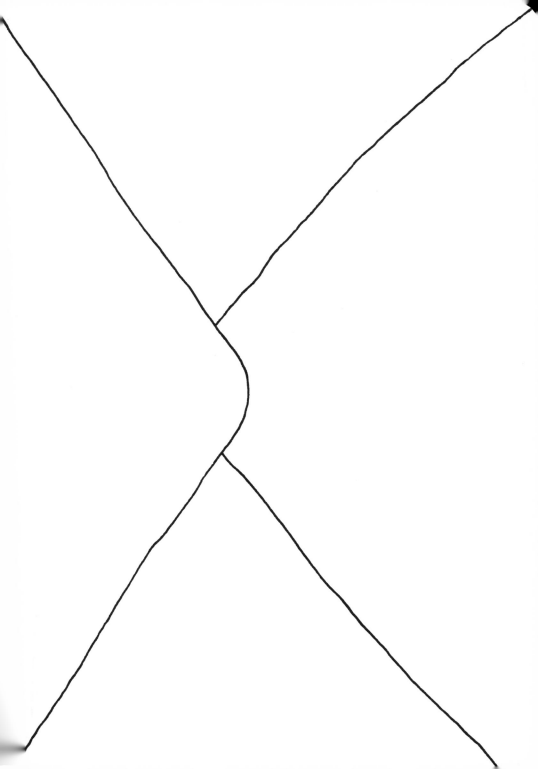

JOURNAL GOLF

1. TEAR OUT PAGE. CRUMPLE INTO A BALL.

2. PLACE JOURNAL INTO A TRIANGLE SHAPE.

3. HIT/KICK THE BALL THROUGH THE TRIANGLE.

這是一本高爾夫球書
1. 撕下這一頁，揉成一團當球
2. 把這本書擺成立三角狀
3. 踢球，或擊球，球必須穿過整本書

make a paper chain.

沿虛線剪下，做成一條紙圈圈

收集水果貼紙（買水果時貼在水果表面的小貼紙），
黏貼在這一頁

COLLECT
FRUIT
STICKERS*
HERE.

* STICKERS YOU FIND ON BOUGHT FRUIT.

COVER THIS PAGE

用辦公室文具把這一頁蓋滿

USING ONLY office SUPPLIES.

BRING THIS BOOK IN THE SHOWER WITH YOU.

帶這本書去洗澡

TIE A STRING TO THE JOURNAL.

GO FOR A WALK, DRAG IT.

拿條繩子綁著這本書，
拖著書去散步。

抓泥土在這裡抹一抹

USE THIS AS A

test Page

FOR PENS, PAINTS, MARKERS, OR ART SUPPLIES.

拿原子筆、顏料、麥克筆，或其他美術用品，在這一頁試寫、試畫。

滴東西在這裡（墨水、顏料，或是茶），闔上書讓顏色印過去。

DRIP
SOMETHING
HERE.
(INK, PAINT, TEA)
CLOSE THE BOOK
TO MAKE A
PRINT.

在這頁縫東西

glue A RANDOM PAGE FROM A NEWSPAPER HERE.

隨便從報紙選一頁黏貼在這裡

這裡讓你寫購物清單

A PLACE FOR YOUR GROCERY LISTS.

COLLECT THE STAMPS OFF
OF ALL YOUR MAIL.

收集你收到的所有郵票

拿出包包裡或口袋裡的東西，描出輪廓線，讓線條互相重疊。

TRACE THE THINGS
IN YOUR BAG (OR POCKETS).
LET THE LINES OVERLAP.

用白色的東西貼滿這一頁

COVER THIS PAGE

WITH WHITE THINGS.

scribble wildly using only borrowed pens.

(document where they were borrowed from.)

隨意亂塗鴉，但只能用借來的鉛筆。（記下這些筆是從哪裡借來的。）

和這本書一起突然來個讓人意想不到的破壞動作

MAKE A SUDDEN, DESTRUCTIVE, UNPREDICTABLE MOVEMENT WITH THE JOURNAL.

搞得亂七八糟，然後整理乾淨

MAKE A MESS, CLEAN IT UP.

DOODLE OVER TOP OF:

在以下這幾頁隨意亂寫：

☐ THE COVER.
封面

☐ THE TITLE PAGE.
書名頁

☐ THE INSTRUCTIONS.
說明頁

☐ THE COPYRIGHT PAGE.
版權頁

FOLD DOWN THE CORNERS OF YOUR FAVORITE PAGES.

在你最喜歡的那幾頁折角做個記號

Page of good thoughts.

蔬菜切塊之後，沾印台墨水印在這裡。

 PRINTS USING AN INK PAD
AND CUT VEGETABLES.

ASK A FRIEND TO DO SOMETHING DESTRUCTIVE TO THIS PAGE. DON'T LOOK.

請朋友破壞這一頁。你不要看。

WRITE CARELESSLY. NOW. 隨便寫點什麼，馬上！

GLUE RANDOM ITEMS HERE.
(i.e., things you find in your couch, on the street, etc.)

在這裡隨便黏點東西，例如在沙發縫裡或街上找到的東西之類的。

tear this page out.

PUT IT IN YOUR POCKET.
PUT IT THROUGH THE WASH.
STICK IT BACK IN.

撕下這一頁，放在衣服口袋裡，把衣服拿去洗，
然後把這頁黏回去。

一次剪破好幾頁

CUT
THROUGH
SEVERAL
LAYERS

Infuse this page with a smell of your choosing.

選一種味道來薰這一頁

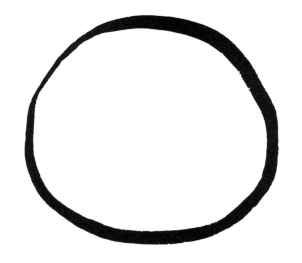

COLOR OUTSIDE
OF THE LINES.

在線條之外的地方著色

閉上眼睛，靠記憶把這些點連起來。

CLOSE YOUR EYES.

CONNECT THE DOTS
FROM MEMORY.

HANG THE JOURNAL IN A PUBLIC PLACE.
INVITE PEOPLE TO DRAW HERE.

把這本書掛在公共場所，請別人在這裡畫畫。

COLLECT YOUR

收集你口袋裡的棉絮、線頭，黏在這裡。

GLUE IT HERE.

↙ ↓ ↓ ↘

POCKET LINT.

畫出手的輪廓

trace YOUR hand.

用膠水畫畫

draw with
GLUE.

在家裡找一些有的沒有的東西，記下這些東西的名稱，創造出色彩繽紛的作品。

SAMPLE VARIOUS SUBSTANCES FOUND IN YOUR HOME.

DOCUMENT WHAT THEY ARE.
CREATE COLOR THEMES.

DOCUMENT A BORING

詳細紀錄一件無聊的事情

EVENT IN DETAIL.

用你的一根（或好幾根）頭髮畫一幅畫

CREATE A DRAWING USING A PIECE (OR SEVERAL PIECES) OF YOUR HAIR.

STICK PHOTO
HERE.

（黏貼照片在此）

glue in a photo of
yourself you dislike.
DEFACE.

貼一張你不好看的照片。把臉塗掉。

（像是棍子、湯匙、繩結、梳子……之類的。）

等你真的真的很生氣的時候，填滿這一頁

fill in this
page when
you are really
ANGRY.

WRITE OR DRAW

用左手寫字或畫畫

WITH YOUR LEFT HAND.

想辦法把這本書穿在身上

FIND A WAY TO WEAR THE JOURNAL.

this page is a sign.
what do you want it to say?

CREATE A NONSTOP LINE.

畫一條不中斷的線

SPACE FOR NEGATIVE COMMENTS.*

在這頁寫下負面的評價 *

(* WHAT IS YOUR INNER CRITIC SAYING?)

（*你的內心是怎麼説的？）

DRAW LINES WITH YOUR PEN OR PENCIL.

LICK YOUR FINGER AND SMEAR THE LINES.

用筆或鉛筆畫線。

舔一下手指，

把線弄糊。

LOSE
THIS
PAGE.

(THROW IT OUT.)
ACCEPT THE LOSS.

失去這一頁。（丟掉這頁。）接受失去的事實。

這一頁寫髒話髒話髒話（也可寫love, kind, good......）

A PAGE for FOUR-LETTER WORDS.

GLUE IN A PAGE FROM A MAGAZINE.

CIRCLE WORDS YOU LIKE.

黏上雜誌裡的一頁，圈出你喜歡的字。

請咬筆在這裡寫字

write with the pen in your mouth.

把你最喜歡的一頁送人

.drawkcab etirW

倒著寫。（鏡像）

紀錄時間的流逝

THIS SPACE IS DEDICATED
這塊空間獻給內心獨白

TO INTERNAL MONOLOGUE.

SCRUB THIS PAGE.

刷刷這一頁

在這本書裡某個地方
寫下一段秘密訊息。

HIDE A SECRET MESSAGE SOMEWHERE IN THIS BOOK.

SLEEP WITH THE JOURNAL.

跟這本書一起睡覺。（在這裡寫下這段經驗。）

(Describe the experience here.)

CLOSE THE JOURNAL.

WRITE/SCRIBBLE SOMETHING ON THE EDGES.

闔上書，在邊邊寫字或畫畫。

WRITE A LIST OF MORE WAYS TO WRECK THIS JOURNAL.

寫下更多做了這本書的方法

1.

2.

3.

4.

5.

6.

7.

8.

9.

10.

11.

12.

STAIN LOG

污漬紀錄

DOODLE OVER TOP OF THIS PAGE ↓↓↓ AND IN THE MARGINS.

在這頁上亂畫，連邊邊也畫滿。

這篇文章一點也不重要，作者寫作的目的其實是要製造一段沒什麼意義的文字，甚至一點意義都沒有，這樣的文字只是讓讀者拿來當作畫布而已，希望這段文字會很像你記憶中的某一本書，這本書是你小時候讀過的，或是你偷偷用蠟筆寫的，可能還有人因為這樣罵過你。

可能是你的第一本課本，因為看到前一位使用者畫了一點點塗鴉，激發你拿起筆在上面亂畫亂塗，這不是你的錯，課本就是要拿來亂畫的，這是課本的天職，你不應該受到責罰，跟課本一樣無聊的東西都應該得到這種下場。

你在讀這段文章嗎？你應該要在這頁上亂畫才對，請不要再讀了！你的機會來了，亂寫亂畫吧。

可能因為是我叫你亂畫，所以你感覺沒那麼想亂畫，既然如此，我命令你立刻停止畫圖！如果你再在這頁上留下一點痕跡，作者本人會禁止你再讀她之後的所有作品，永遠都不准！（至少是她有繼續寫書的話，那可能也是一段很長很長的時間。）

你還有很多事情可以做，比亂畫這一頁更有好處，比方說去看牙醫啦，清理冰箱啦，洗窗戶啦，打掃床底啦，讀完普魯斯特作品全集啦，按照筆劃順序整理食物啦，進行聚合物合成的科學研究以及其對世界的影響啦，按照大小整理信封啦，數一數你手上有多少張紙啦，確認每一雙襪子都是成對的啦，記下你口袋裡有哪些線頭啦（喔對了，你在這本書前面已經做過了），回電給你媽啦，學習一種新語言啦，錄下你睡覺的聲音啦，移動傢俱把家裡變成公車站啦，實驗你以前沒試過的新坐姿啦，原地慢跑一小時啦，假裝你是密探啦，裝飾冰箱內部啦，用粉筆在牆上畫一道假門啦，跟你的動物鄰居聊一聊啦，為未來可能得到的獎寫一篇得獎感言啦，走到街角的商店啦（愈慢愈好喔），寫封信給你的郵差說些好話鼓勵他啦，在圖書館借來的書裡放一封秘密紙條啦，做點鍛練手指的運動啦，打扮成你最喜歡的作家啦，聞聞看你鼻子裡的味道啦，默背史傳克和懷特寫的《寫作風格的要素》啦，坐在前廊上手裡舉個牌子寫著「愛鳥的人就按喇叭」啦，在紙上寫下你生活中認識的植物啦，聞一下這本書啦，睡一下啦，假裝你是有名的太空人啦，都很好吧。

想辦法把這兩頁連結在一起

FIGURE OUT A WAY TO ATTACH THESE TWO PAGES TOGETHER.

把這頁拿到髒車上抹一抹

RUB THIS PAGE ON A DIRTY CAR.

COLLECT THE LETTER "W" HERE.

收集字母W

✗COLLECT
DEAD
BUGS
HERE.

收集死掉的蟲子

用鉛筆咚咚咚敲擊這頁

DRUM ON THIS PAGE WITH PENCILS.

FLOAT THIS PAGE.

讓這頁漂起來

想辦法冷凍這頁

FIGURE OUT A WAY TO **FREEZE** THIS PAGE.

HIDE THIS PAGE IN YOUR NEIGHBOR'S YARD.

把這頁藏在鄰居家的院子

把這本書從陡坡上滾下去

ROLL THE JOURNAL DOWN A LARGE HILL.

SELL THIS PAGE.

賣了這一頁

把這本書變成一隻鞋

把這本書滑過（這頁朝下）走廊

SLIDE THE JOURNAL
(THIS PAGE FACE-DOWN),
DOWN A LONG HALLWAY.

把有顏色的東西擠壓在這頁上

SQUIRT LIQUID HERE (TRY USING YOUR MOUTH).

在這頁噴液體（試著用嘴巴噴）

在這頁上貼滿膠帶（貼出有創意的圖形）

COVER THIS PAGE IN TAPE

(CREATE SOME KIND OF PATTERN).

描畫你的腳趾頭

TRACE YOUR TOES.

不玩了
這一頁你自己搞